The Boy
Who Wasn't
There

When I heard this story for the first time many years ago I didn't believe it. I thought it was too strange, too unusual to be true. I only accepted that which was reasonable and logical.

But now I'm not so certain anymore. As a matter of fact the older I get, the more I begin to trust the things which cannot always be explained.

The Boy
Who Wasn't
There

A mystery by

HANS WILHELM

SCHOLASTIC
HARDCOVER

SCHOLASTIC INC.
NEW YORK

"Surely it is a little conceited of us to suppose
we are the only spiritual inhabitants of this world?"
—Robertson Davies

Copyright © 1993 by Hans Wilhelm, Inc.
All rights reserved. Published by Scholastic Inc.
SCHOLASTIC HARDCOVER is a registered trademark of
Scholastic Inc.

No part of this publication may be reproduced in whole or in part,
or stored in a retrieval system, or transmitted in any form
or by any means, electronic, mechanical, photocopying, recording, or otherwise,
without written permission of the publisher.
For information regarding permission, write to Scholastic Inc.,
730 Broadway, New York, NY 10003.

Library of Congress Cataloging-in-Publication Data

Wilhelm, Hans, 1945-
The boy who wasn't there / by Hans Wilhelm.
p.   cm.
Summary: A mysterious boy who seems to come and go without warning
leads lonely Sarah to the new friend which is her heart's desire.
ISBN 0-590-46635-6
[1. Ghosts—Fiction. 2. Friendship—Fiction.] I. Title.
PZ7.W64816Bo   1993
[E]—dc20   92-29874
                                            CIP
                                            AC

12 11 10 9 8 7 6 5 4 3 2 1   3 4 5 6 7 8/9
Printed in the U.S.A.   36
First Scholastic printing, November 1993

The illustrations in this book were done
with watercolors on Strathmore Bristol paper.
Book design by David Turner.

I
THE MYSTERIOUS STRANGER

It all began many years ago on a cold and windy day in
December. The waves were beating against the shore of the
rocky coast of New England.

Sarah was sitting in the bay window of a big house, looking
out at the gray sky. She was playing with her friends, Punch
and Polly. They were puppets.

Sarah wished she had a real friend to play with. But there
were no other children nearby, and she had not made any friends
at boarding school either.

Now that she was home for Christmas vacation, she felt very lonely.

"I want to go out!" said Punch. "I want to go to the beach."

"It's too cold and windy," Polly said.

"Nonsense!" Punch said. "The wind is fun. Let's go."

Sarah always sided with Punch, so she took the puppets
and went outside.

The seagulls were screaming above her as she made her way down to the shore. Usually Sarah liked to play on the rocks. But today she didn't feel like it. She sat down and pulled the coat closer around her. The empty beach made her feel even more lonely than before.

Sarah picked up Punch and Polly, hoping they would cheer her up. But now they only looked at her with their lifeless wooden faces.

"Silly toys!" she said, and threw them down.

With a stick, Sarah began to draw pictures in the sand. First she drew a picture of herself. Then very carefully she drew another figure right next to it.

Suddenly Sarah had the eerie feeling that somebody was watching her.

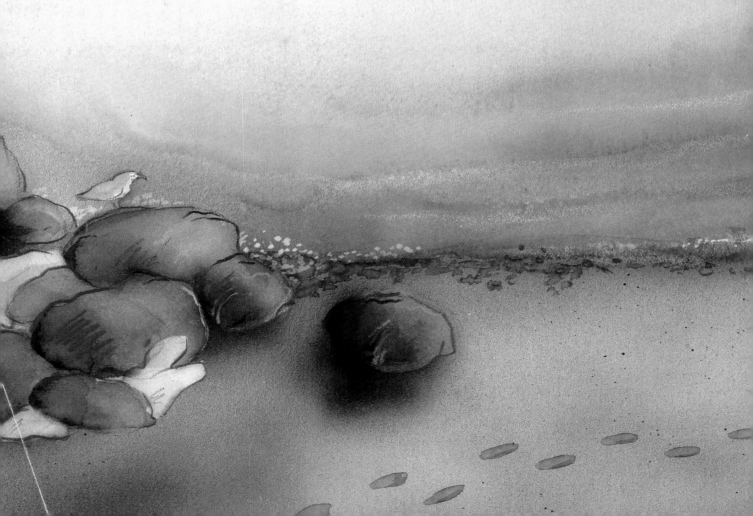

"What a nice picture of you and your friend," said a voice next to her.

With a jerk, Sarah turned around and found herself looking right into the face of a boy she had never seen before.

"Who are you?" she asked. "Where did you come from?"

The boy didn't answer. He just smiled. Then finally he said, "Don't worry. It will turn out all right. You will have a best friend very soon."

Sarah felt the blood rush to her face. She turned away.

"Oh really?" she said angrily. "What do you know about it? One thing is certain: It won't be you. I don't like boys who like to scare people."

She waited for him to speak.

But when Sarah looked up, the boy was gone. He was nowhere to be seen. Where could he have gone so fast? Was he hiding behind the rocks?

"Hey! Come here!" Sarah cried. "Where are you?"

Sarah got up and searched the rocks. But she didn't find the boy anywhere. What's more, the only footprints in the sand were her own.

Did I imagine it all? Sarah wondered.

Neither the wind nor the waves would give her an answer.

II
THE VISIT

It was just before Christmas when Sarah saw
the boy for the second time. Her parents had
gone out and she was alone in the house, putting
on a puppet show in the large drawing room.
Suddenly he was there, standing behind the chairs.

Sarah was stunned. She had not seen nor heard
him enter.

"You must come with me," he said. His face
was pale and very serious.

Sarah was too surprised to speak.

"You must come with me," the boy said again.
"Bring your puppets. I need your help. Please."

Sarah started to object, but there was something
in his voice that stopped her. She knew she had
to go with him. She got her coat, picked up her
puppets, and followed the boy out of the house.

Silently Sarah walked behind the stranger. Where was he taking her? What was wrong with him? Why didn't he wear a coat in this icy weather?

They walked for a long while until they came to a very poor neighborhood. Sarah had never been in this part of town.

Finally they came to an old rundown house.

They climbed an outside staircase to the second floor, and the boy motioned Sarah to open the door.

There was a single room. Sarah could see a woman sitting beside a small bed. In the bed a girl seemed to be asleep.

Then Sarah noticed that the woman had been crying.

The boy pointed to the little girl. "Show her your puppets," he said. He looked at Sarah with such pleading eyes that she stepped closer to the bed.

Sarah put the puppets on her hands. In the warm glow of the lamp they jumped to life.

"Hi! I'm Punch!"

"Hi! I'm Polly!"

The little girl opened her eyes and tried to raise her head to get a better view. She began to smile, and finally she even laughed as the puppets played one joke after another.

Seeing the little girl smiling and laughing brought more tears to the woman's eyes. She hugged and kissed her.

"Oh, my darling, your terrible fever is gone. Thank God. I was so worried. But now you will be well again. I know it."

Then the woman turned to Sarah. "Who are you? How did you get here? How can I ever thank you for what you've done?"

"My name is Sarah. And this boy brought me here."

Sarah turned around to look for him. But nobody was there.

"A boy? What boy?" asked the woman. "I don't understand. We just moved to this town. We don't know any boys here."

Sarah was confused. She looked around her, wondering what was happening. Where had he gone again?

"But there! That's him!" Sarah pointed to a framed photograph on the table next to the girl's bed. "That's the boy!"

"Him?" said the woman, and took the photograph into her hands. She looked at it for a while and said, "You say he brought you here?"

"Yes, he did. He made me come with him and asked me to bring my puppets, too."

"Then it must be true," the woman said quietly. "That sounds like Allan."

"His name is Allan?" asked Sarah. "Who is he?"

And then the woman began to tell the story of Allan.

III
ALLAN

"It was about two years ago," said the woman. "We lived in a village, a bit farther up the coast. One day there was a terrible storm. Many people had to leave their homes. But there are always some who like to stay on the shore to watch the fierce waves. That day one of them was my son Allan. He was an excellent swimmer and loved the ocean.

"Two other boys were there, too, climbing on some rocks. The waves were thundering around them, splashing high in the air.

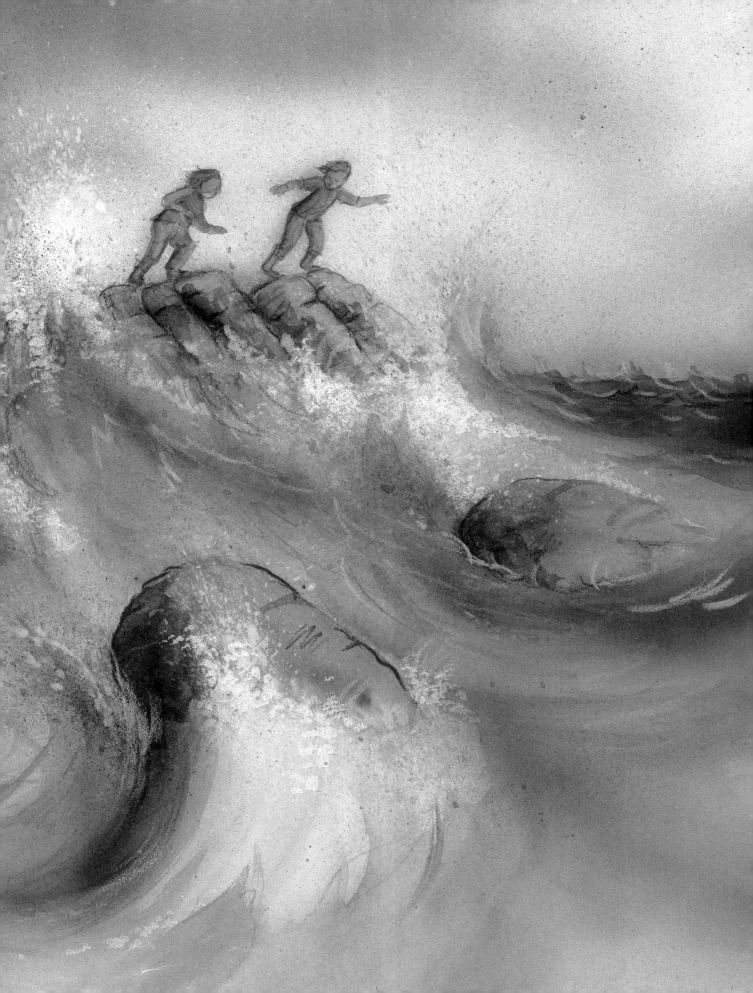

"Suddenly the water subsided for a moment, only to form one big, enormous wave. It was taller than a house. With a roar, the wave came rushing toward the shore, rolling over the two boys and crashing against the seawall.

"When it was gone, only one boy was left on the rocks.

"The people on the shore could not believe what had happened. They screamed and shouted, but no one knew what to do.

"Meanwhile, the boy who was washed over was rapidly drifting out to sea.

"Allan took off his boots and jumped into the cold water. He swam toward the boy, but the strong current kept pulling him away.

"It seemed like hours before the boy was finally saved. Another big wave came and pushed him back to the shore. He was lucky."

"And Allan?" asked Sarah. "What happened to him?"

"We searched for him everywhere," the woman said. "But we never found him. He never came back."

The woman looked at the photograph again, then gently placed it back on the table.

EPILOGUE

Sarah hoped she would see Allan again some day. Often she went to the beach to look for him, but she never saw him.

After a while she began to visit the girl who was Allan's sister. Her name was Angela. Soon they became best friends. Sarah's wish had come true — just as Allan had predicted.

Later, the girls went to school and college together. They each got married. And when they had their first sons, they called them both
ALLAN.